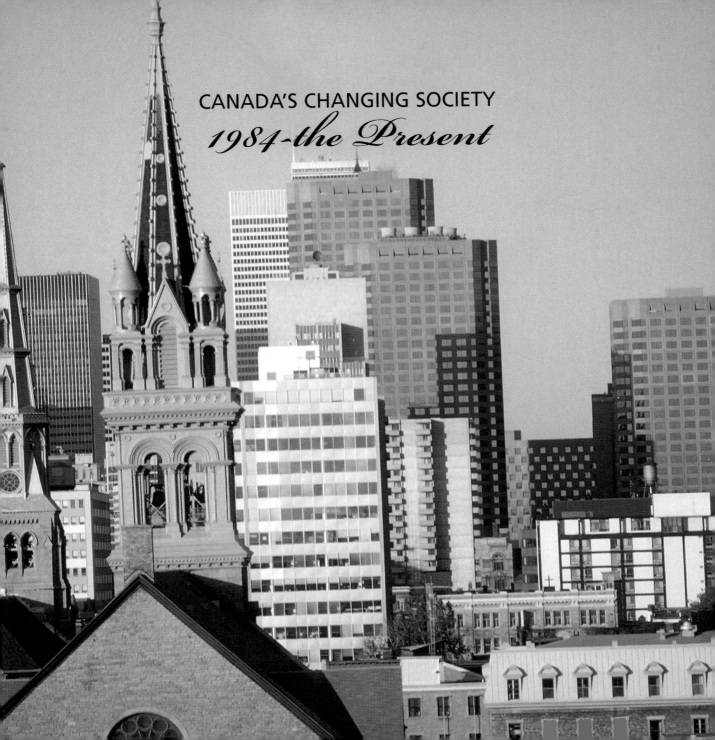

CANADA'S CHANGING SOCIETY
1984-the Present

TITLE LIST

CANADA'S CHANGING SOCIETY
1984-the Present

BY
SHEILA NELSON

MASON CREST PUBLISHERS
PHILADELPHIA

Mason Crest Publishers Inc.
370 Reed Road
Broomall, Pennsylvania 19008
(866) MCP-BOOK (toll free)

First printing
1 2 3 4 5 6 7 8 9 10

        Library of Congress Cataloging-in-Publication Data

Nelson, Sheila.
  Canada's changing society, 1984 – the present / by Sheila Nelson.
     p. cm. — (How Canada became Canada)
  Includes index.
  ISBN 1-4222-0009-4   ISBN 1-4222-0000-0 (series)
 1. Canada—History—1945——Juvenile literature. 2. Canada—Politics and government—1980——Juvenile literature. I. Title.
  F1034.2.N412 2006
  971.104—dc22
                   2005016556

Produced by Harding House Publishing Service, Inc.
www.hardinghousepages.com
Interior design by MK Bassett-Harvey.
Cover design by Dianne Hodack.
Printed in Hashemite Kingdom of Jordan.

CONTENTS

INTRODUCTION

by David Bercuson

Every country's history is distinct, and so is Canada's. Although Canada is often said to be a pale imitation of the United States, it has a unique history that has created a modern North American nation on its own path to democracy and social justice. This series explains how that happened.

Canada's history is rooted in its climate, its geography, and in its separate political development. Virtually all of Canada experiences long, dark, and very cold winters with copious amounts of snowfall. Canada also spans several distinct geographic regions, from the rugged western mountain ranges on the Pacific coast to the forested lowlands of the St. Lawrence River Valley and the Atlantic tidewater region.

Canada's regional divisions were complicated by the British conquest of New France at the end of the Seven Years' War in 1763. Although Britain defeated France, the French were far more numerous in Canada than the British. Britain was thus forced to recognize French Canadian rights to their own language, religion, and culture. That recognition is now enshrined in the Canadian Constitution. It has made Canada a democracy that values group rights alongside individual rights, with official French/English bilingualism as a key part of the Canadian character.

During the American Revolution, Canadians chose to stay British. After the Revolution, they provided refuge to tens of thousands of Americans who, for one reason or another, did not follow George Washington, Benjamin Franklin, or the other founders of the United States who broke with Britain.

Democracy in Canada under the British Crown evolved more slowly than it did in the United States. But in the early nineteenth century, slavery was outlawed in the

British Empire, and as a result, also in Canada. Thus Canada never experienced civil war or government-imposed racial segregation.

From these few, brief examples, it is clear that Canada's history differs considerably from that of the United States. And yet today, Canada is a true North American democracy in its own right. Canadians will profit from a better understanding of how their country was shaped—and Americans may learn much about their own country by studying the story of Canada.

Modern Canada

One

THE MULRONEY YEARS

Late in July of 1984, Prime Minister John Turner faced Progressive Conservation Party leader Brian Mulroney in a debate. Turner had served as prime minister for less than a month, stepping in as leader of the Liberal Party after the resignation of Prime Minister Pierre Trudeau. The general election was scheduled for September. During the first weeks of the campaign, Turner and the Liberals looked strong. Then, Mulroney struck back, hitting hard. Canadians started to think about the things they had not liked about the Liberals during the years they had been in power.

The Turner-Mulroney debate of July 1984 was an important turning point in the election campaign. During the debate, Mulroney attacked the Liberal Party's practice of *patronage*, specifically the seventy-nine political appointments Turner had made shortly after becoming prime minister, fulfilling a promise he had made to Pierre Trudeau. When Turner responded to Mulroney's criticism by saying he had

Patronage refers to appointments or privileges a politician can give to supporters.

Tariffs *are duties levied by a government on goods, usually imports.*

had no choice, Mulroney refused to back down. "You did have an option!" Mulroney declared, brimming with righteous indignation. "You had an option to say 'no,' sir, and you chose to say 'yes' to the old attitudes and the old stories of the

Brian Mulroney and his wife Mila

Liberal Party." When Turner tried to repeat that he had had no option but to make the appointments, Mulroney shot back that if true, that was simply an admission of weak leadership.

Canadians were wildly enthusiastic about Brian Mulroney. They overwhelmingly chose Mulroney in the September 4 general election. The Progressive Conservative Party swept the election, winning 211 of 282 seats.

A Change in Leadership

By 1984, when Pierre Trudeau announced he would step down as prime minister, the Liberal Party had led Canada for about twenty years—not including the few months Joe Clark spent as prime minister from 1979 to 1980. During those years, the national debt had soared, and the economy had stagnated. People had tired of Liberal leadership and were ready for a change. Brian Mulroney, with his suave charm, appealed to Canadians.

In his early years as prime minister, Mulroney worked to create closer ties with the United States. Canada's relationship with the United States had become strained during Trudeau's administration, but Mulroney wanted to create a stronger bond with Canada's southern neighbor. Reducing Canada's debt was another of Mulroney's early priorities. He accomplished this by making massive spending cuts, breaking several election campaign promises to increase spending on certain social programs.

Mulroney's desire to form a closer relationship with the United States led him to introduce a free trade agreement between Canada and the United States. Free trade meant no *tariffs* on trade items covered by the deal. Since Confederation in 1867, no political candidate who had endorsed free trade with the United States had ever been elected. During the 1984 election campaign, Mulroney stated that he was against the idea of free trade, although no one else had discussed the issue. Several years after his election as prime minister, Mulroney reversed his earlier position and began talks with U.S. representatives about the possibility of free trade.

The Free Trade Agreement became the defining issue of the 1988 general election. The Liberal Party and the New Democratic Party (NDP) both opposed the Free Trade Agreement, along with many labor unions. The Conservatives, on the other hand, believed the agreement would be a good thing

*A **premier** is the leader of a Canadian province.*

*
Veto power is the ability to reject legislation.*

for Canada and for Canadians. Many Canadians agreed, and Mulroney was reelected with a majority government. On January 1, 1989, the Free Trade Agreement took effect. The deal did increase cross-border trade, although it remained controversial.

The Meech Lake Accord

One of Mulroney's main goals as prime minister was to "bring Québec into the constitution." Although Québec was governed by the constitution, brought into effect in 1982, no Québec *premier* had agreed to sign the document.

In 1987, Mulroney met with the ten provincial premiers at a conference center on Meech Lake, Québec. At the meetings, Mulroney proposed a series of constitutional amendments. The Meech Lake Accord, as the amendments were called, gave the provinces much greater freedoms than the current constitution, including granting each provincial premier *veto power* for future constitutional changes.

Another major point of the accord was that it labeled Québec as a "distinct society." While many believed this was simply an official recognition of what had always been true and Canadians had always known, others feared Québec would be given too many powers and freedoms as a result. For one thing, not only did the accord recognize Québec as a distinct society, it also confirmed "the role of the legislature and Government of Quebec to preserve and promote the distinct identity of Quebec." This clause was open ended, and critics claimed the Québec government could interpret it however they wanted, thereby, in effect, allowing Québec to govern itself apart from the laws of Canada.

A political cartoon portrays Mulroney's position in the Meech Lake Accord.

The Free Trade Agreement increased trade between Canada and the United States.

The Meech Lake Accord said that Québec was a "distinct society."

Other regions of Canada also objected to the distinct society clause, protesting they too were distinct societies within Canada. Of course Québec was distinct, they said, but no more so than Newfoundland fishing communities or Prairie farm towns. The problem came, however, not so much from naming Québec a distinct society, but from

The Meech Lake Accord, signed by Prime Minister Mulroney and the province premiers

then granting that province extra powers not given to the rest of Canada.

At the original Meech Lake meetings in June of 1987, all of the ten provincial premiers signed the accord, along with Prime Minister Mulroney. Each of the premiers was given three years to debate the constitutional amendments in their provincial parliaments and approve the accord.

Former prime minister Pierre Trudeau was so opposed to the Meech Lake Accord

that he came out of retirement—breaking his self-imposed silence—to speak out against the proposed constitutional amendments. Trudeau claimed the accord would severely weaken the federal government, giving too much power to the provinces. He also believed the accord set a dangerous

The Manitoba Legislative Assembly

A **precedent** is an action or decision that can be used as an example for later action or decision.

Mohawk in traditional costume

Modern-day Mohawk women stand next to a statue memorializing their people's history.

18

precedent by dividing Canada into French-speakers who were mainly in Québec and English-speakers who were primarily in the rest of Canada. This, together with calling Québec a "distinct society" and giving it special powers, divided Canada in a way Trudeau thought it should not be divided.

Before the 1990 deadline arrived, three of the provinces—Newfoundland, New Brunswick, and Manitoba—had elected new premiers, premiers who had not been part of the original Meech Lake talks. Early in June of 1990, just a few weeks before the deadline, Mulroney held another conference with the premiers. There, he finally convinced them all to discuss the issue with their provincial legislatures to pass the accord. Mulroney was thrilled with the outcome of the meeting, and bragged to a Toronto newspaper that he had gambled on successfully pressuring the premiers into agreeing by holding the conference so close to the

Crisis in Oka

In 1989, the town of Oka, Québec, decided to expand its golf course. Unfortunately, the proposed site of the golf course was a Mohawk burial ground and sacred birch grove. Protests increased in early 1990, as the Mohawk barricaded the roads to the site and set up a barbed-wire fence in front of the forest. When the Québec police arrived to confront the Mohawk, a clash broke out that left one police officer dead. Finally, the Canadian army was called in. The army arrived with tanks and soldiers and slowly pushed through the Mohawk barriers. In late September of 1990, months after the standoff began, the Mohawk surrendered. The golf course was never expanded, although the Mohawk land claims had not been resolved.

Wholesale means to be sold to merchants for resale.

deadline. The premiers were furious at Mulroney's comments; he had made them look foolish by claiming to have manipulated them. Many Canadians were also outraged, and public opinion of the Meech Lake Accord fell.

The GST affected small Canadian businesses like this one.

The premiers who had not already done so presented their provincial legislature with the accord and began debates. In Manitoba, Premier Gary Filmon put forward the accord for a vote. This was simply a preliminary vote; to begin debates, he needed the approval of all members of the Manitoba Legislative Assembly. In most cases, such a vote would be quick and easy. In this case, one member, Elijah Harper, a Cree Native, objected to the Meech Lake Accord because it did not discuss First Nations' rights. When Harper was asked whether he would vote to introduce the accord for debate, he held up an eagle feather and said, "No, Mr. Speaker." For days, the Speaker of the House repeated his question, and each time Harper responded in the same way, accompanied by cheers from First Nations' protesters in the gallery. Harper and the other First Nations people did not care so much about giving Québec distinct society status; but they felt the First Nations deserved such status as well.

When Newfoundland's premier, Clyde Wells, realized Harper would probably be successful in blocking the accord, he dropped debates on the issue in Newfoundland's House of Assembly as well. Wells had always been reluctant to agree, but had consented to hold debates on the ac-

cord. As the deadline grew closer, however, Mulroney continued to pressure Wells to pass the accord. Wells felt increasingly manipulated and uncomfortable. He believed he had compromised too many of his beliefs. Finally, the pressure tactics and manipulation were too much for him. He and the Newfoundland House of Assembly agreed not to vote on the Meech Lake Accord, and in doing so, effectively killed the accord. Newfoundland bore the brunt of Québec's blame along with Mulroney, since the federal government had offered to make a deal with Elijah Harper to resolve the crisis—but only if Newfoundland first agreed to pass the accord, and Newfoundland refused.

Goods and Services Tax

In 1989, not long after his reelection, Mulroney proposed the idea of creating a national sales tax. Canadians were instantly outraged at the idea. The goods and services tax (GST) would replace a manufacturers' sales tax charged to manufacturers on *wholesale* goods, but this did not satisfy the many who believed the GST would hurt consumers. Those in Alberta—the only province who did not already have a provincial sales tax (PST)—made some of the strongest protests against the GST. Many of Conservative supporters in the province abandoned the party to back the recently formed Reform Party of Canada. The party had been established in 1987 to uphold western Canadian interests, since many felt the federal government too often ignored western concerns in favor of issues affecting the central provinces.

One of the things critics objected to was the complexity of the GST. The 7 percent tax would be applied to certain things—those considered "unnecessary," such as snack food or shipping costs—but the list of taxable and nontaxable items often made no sense to Canadians. For example, GST applied to convenience foods, but not always if they were sold to be eaten later; in this way, a customer would pay GST on a purchase of one or two doughnuts but not on a purchase of at least half a dozen. Also, PST was not always applied to the same items as was GST, further confusing the issue. Small-business owners, too, hated the thought of the new tax. GST would mean hundreds of pages of new regulations to learn and mountains of paperwork to complete.

Despite the unpopularity of the proposed GST, Mulroney and the Conservatives continued to push it through legislation. The Liberal Party and the New Democratic Party (NDP), the other parties with elected Members of Parliament (MP), tried to fight the tax, but the Conservatives were determined.

To become law, both the House of Commons and the Senate needed to pass the GST legislation. Since the House of Commons had many more Conservative members than any other party, the tax finally passed at that level. The Senate, however, was dominated by the Liberal Party, which blocked the proposed tax. Mulroney responded by digging up an old law—one most Canadians didn't know existed—that allowed him to temporarily bring in eight new Conservative Senators to give the Conservative Party the majority. The angry Liberals then *filibustered* for several months before finally allowing the tax to pass into law. The new GST took effect on January 1, 1991.

Prime Minister Mulroney had introduced several controversial issues during his first years in office. Canadians protested his Free Trade Agreement with the United States, but most came to accept it. The Meech Lake Accord had been even more controversial, and the anticipated constitutional amendment, intended to satisfy Québec, was killed by Manitoba MP Elijah Harper and New-

Canadian consumers could avoid paying sales tax by buying a dozen doughnuts rather than one or two.

foundland premier Clyde Wells. In spite of the debates over free trade and Meech Lake, Mulroney was reelected in 1988. The national sales tax, the GST, truly angered many Canadians, though. Mulroney found his popularity slipping badly. Many felt his only contributions to Canada had been high taxes and an increasingly unhappy Québec.

Filibustered means made long speeches on the floor of the legislature to prevent something from coming to a vote.

During the early 1990s, the "Québec issue" continued to dominate Canada. Mulroney had not yet given up on finding a constitutional amendment Québec and the majority of Canadians would accept. In 1992, he would begin another series of meetings to draft a new constitutional amendment.

Codfishing was once a thriving business in Newfoundland.

The Death of the Cod Fishery

In 1497, when John Cabot discovered Newfoundland, he reported the fish were so plentiful they could be scooped up by the basketful. Canadians thought the cod would be inexhaustible. In the mid-1980s, however, inshore fishermen, those who fished in small boats close to home, reported a dramatic decrease in their catches. By 1989, everyone could see clearly that there was much less cod than in past years. The Newfoundland government put stricter limits on the cod fishery, but the limits did not help. In 1992, the minister of fisheries, John Crosbie, declared a ban on the entire cod fishery. The ban would last at least two years. Crosbie and others hoped this would give the cod a chance to rebuild their populations. Tens of thousands of Newfoundland fishermen were suddenly out of work, outraged at the small compensation package the government offered them. By the early twenty-first century, despite continuing bans, the fishery had still not recovered, and scientists believed overfishing had permanently disrupted the cod populations.

In the 1990s, Québec continued to play a major role in Canadian politics.

Two

CONTINUING STRUGGLES WITH QUÉBEC

On October 26, 1992, Canadians went to the polls in a *referendum* to vote on the Charlottetown Accord. The Charlottetown Accord was an agreement finalized on August 28, 1992, that would amend the Canadian constitution. Similar to the Meech Lake Accord in many ways, the Charlottetown Accord attempted to address Québec's dissatisfaction with the Canadian constitution. Prime Minister Mulroney hoped this time Canadians would agree with the amendment. On October 26, however, over 54 percent of Canadians voted against the accord. The "Son of Meech" had died like its father.

The Charlottetown Accord

Mulroney's popularity had dived sharply during the GST debates. Still, the prime minister felt he needed to accomplish one of his major goals before he could leave office. That goal was to bring Québec into the constitution.

In 1982, René Lévesque, Québec's premier, had refused to sign the new Canadian constitution, claiming the other

*A **referendum** is a vote by an entire electorate on a question put before it by a government or similar body.*

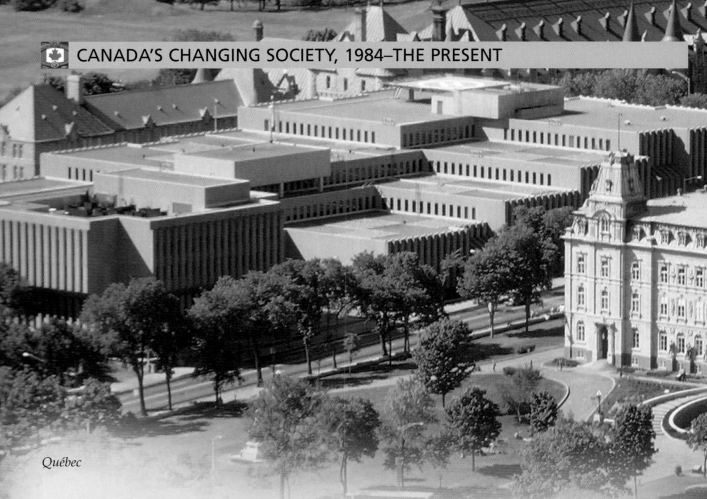

Québec

provinces and the federal government had abandoned his province. Mulroney's earlier attempt to satisfy Québec with the Meech Lake Accord had ended when Newfoundland's premier, Clyde Wells, refused to call a vote before the issue. Elijah Harper, a Cree MP from Manitoba, had also blocked the vote in that province by refusing to give his approval to let the accord pass into the debate phase of the legislative process.

The Charlottetown Accord was intended to be a compromise. It was similar to the Meech Lake Accord, but had several differences. For one thing, the Meech Lake Accord had angered the First Nations people, because it failed to address Native concerns. The Charlottetown Accord affirmed that

"the Aboriginal peoples of Canada have the inherent right of self-government within Canada," but would allow several years for the details of self-government to be worked out. The accord also included the "Canada Clause," a statement of Canadian values. Included in the Canada Clause were multiculturalism, gender equality, Québec's distinct society, and the right of both Québec and First Nations to promote their languages and cultures.

Although many politicians agreed on the Charlottetown Accord, Canadians were not convinced. Some disliked the accord simply because Mulroney was the one promoting it; Mulroney had become extremely unpopular after he had instituted the GST. Many objected to the fact they were being asked to accept or reject the accord as a whole. While most liked parts of the accord, many disagreed with some sections of it. They were annoyed they had no way to choose only certain parts of the accord and no way to let the government know how they really felt.

Former prime minister Pierre Trudeau, who had come out of retirement to speak out against the Meech Lake Accord, came forward again to condemn the Charlottetown Accord. Trudeau was especially angry that the Liberal Party—his party—had officially endorsed the accord. He felt this ac-

Pierre Trudeau

cord had many of the same problems as Meech Lake, specifically that it weakened the federal government too much and gave too much power to the provinces. "They have made a mess and this mess deserves a big No!" Trudeau proclaimed.

To pass into law, the Charlottetown Accord needed to be approved by the majority of Canadians in a national referendum. A majority was needed on a national level, but it was also required on a provincial level. In other words, most voters in each province needed to support the accord; if the voters of any province did not give the accord a majority vote, the accord would die. At a national level, the constitutional amendment received less than 50 percent of Canadian votes, and at a provincial level the accord died as well. Seven of the twelve provinces and territories voted "no," including Québec. Some blamed Mulroney's unpopularity, while others believed Trudeau's opinion had influenced Canadians' vote.

*Someone who is a **separatist** favors breaking away from the ruling government.*

***Sovereignty** refers to being politically independent.*

Separatism and the Bloc Québécois

Canadians had had many reasons for voting against the Charlottetown Accord. While Québec's premier, Robert Bourassa, had campaigned for the accord, other Québécois had been against it. The provincial *separatist* party, the Parti Québécois, along with the recently formed federal separatist party, the Bloc Québécois, argued against the accord because they felt it did not do enough for Québec or give the province enough power. Many separatists felt approving the Charlottetown Accord would be giving up on *sovereignty* for Québec.

Premier Bourassa was a member of the Liberal Party and was not a separatist. He campaigned hard for both the Meech Lake Accord and the Charlottetown Accord because he feared

A New Political Party

In 1990, after the defeat of the Meech Lake Accord, a number of federal Québec politicians from both the Progressive Conservative Party and the Liberal Party came together to form a new party, the Bloc Québécois. The purpose of the Bloc Québécois was to work toward sovereignty for Québec. This was also the goal of the Parti Québécois, and the two often worked closely together, coordinating their efforts at federal (Bloc Québécois) and provincial (Parti Québécois) levels.

if they failed, the Québécois people might be prompted to choose sovereignty over remaining a part of Canada.

After Canadians voted against the Charlottetown Accord, separatism began to take hold in Québec to a much greater extent. Many Québécois felt the federal government had let them down, and they had lost faith in the possibility of future constitutional reforms favoring Québec.

Mulroney Steps Down

The referendum on the Charlottetown Accord made Brian Mulroney even more unpopular. Not only had he introduced the hated GST, but he had also failed to satisfy the Québec people; at the end of 1992, Québec separatism was more of a threat to Canadian unity than ever before. In February of 1993, Mulroney announced his resignation, effective in June.

32

Former Canadian prime ministers. Kim Campbell is in the center.

In June, at the Progressive Conservative Party leadership convention, Kim Campbell was chosen to succeed Mulroney as party leader. Consequently, Campbell became prime minister on June 25, 1993. Campbell was at first very popular among Canadians. She was the first female prime minister, and many hoped she would be able to improve the Conservative Party image.

Campbell did not have much time to gain the approval of Canadians. By law, an election needed to be held at least every five

Kim Campbell's Popularity Slips

Some believed Kim Campbell never really had a chance. She stepped in for Brian Mulroney, who had left office as one of the most hated prime ministers in history—a hatred that would slowly die with time. Nevertheless, she did not help herself. Canadians thought she was arrogant, earning her the chant, "Kim, Kim, you're just like him!" Probably her worst campaign move, though, was an ad mocking Jean Chrétien's facial paralysis, caused by an attack of Bell's Palsy in his youth. Hours after the ad began airing, Campbell realized her mistake and cancelled it. Many Canadians saw the worst segments of it in news reports, however. Chrétien responded calmly: "Last night the Conservative party reached a new low. They tried to make fun of the way I look. God gave me a physical defect. I have accepted that since I was a kid." Canadians, already disgusted with the Conservative Party, chose Chrétien and the Liberals to lead the country.

years, and that time was almost up. When the general election was held four months later, on October 25, the Progressive Conservative Party was almost completely destroyed. From 169 seats just after the last election, the Conservatives fell to only 2 seats, an almost 99 percent loss. Even Campbell lost her own Vancouver seat.

The Liberal Party took control of the House of Commons, and party leader Jean Chrétien became prime minister. The remainder of the House seats was split mostly

The MacPatriation Brothers

Political cartoon portraying Trudeau and Jean Chrétien

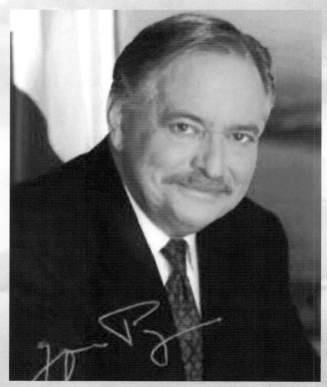

Jacques Parizeau

between the Bloc Québécois and the Reform Party. The NDP had also lost many of their seats, dropping from 43 to 9. The separatist Bloc Québécois, which had not even existed at the time of the last election, became the official opposition party.

During the election campaign, Chrétien had promised to get rid of GST. After he became prime minister, however, the Liberal Party determined that GST had helped to significantly decrease Canada's national debt and had become an essential part of the Canadian economy. Many people criticized Chrétien for this change of attitude, but he did quickly earn a reputation for being careful and practical in his decisions.

Referendum on Québec

In 1980, Québec had held a referendum on whether to consider the option of separating

from the rest of Canada and seeking sovereignty. The "no" side of the issue had won by nearly 60 percent, and the leaders of the separatist movement had concluded the time was not yet right for Québec sovereignty. In September of 1994, the Liberal leadership of Québec faced the Parti Québécois in a provincial election. Daniel Johnson had only served as premier for a few months, having replaced Robert Bourassa who had resigned in January. Many of the Québec people were unhappy with the Liberal leadership in Québec. They turned instead to Jacques Parizeau of the Bloc Québécois. While Canadians in the rest of Canada feared a vote for the Bloc Québécois meant a vote for Québec sovereignty, many Québécois did not see the issue in the same way. They felt they were voting for change, not separation from Canada, and knew they would have the chance to voice their opinions on sovereignty during the referendum Parizeau had promised.

Parizeau and the Bloc Québécois easily won the provincial election and called a referendum for the next year, to be held on October 30, 1995. The Québec people would be asked to vote yes or no on the question: "Do you agree that Quebec should become sovereign after having made a formal offer to Canada for a new economic and political partnership within the scope of the bill respecting the future of Quebec and of the agreement signed on June 12, 1995?" The agreement referred to was a commitment to sovereignty signed by the three separatist parties—Bloc Québécois, Parti Québécois, and Action Démocratique du Québec.

The weeks before the referendum were tense in Canada. Polls showed the yes and no sides were holding almost even, with some polls showing a greater majority on

Québec's coast

the separatist, yes side. Chrétien and the federal government made a massive, last-minute effort to try and influence Québec voters. A huge rally was held in Montréal, attended by people from all across Canada. Chrétien spoke to the Québec people over the television, promising them constitutional concessions. Lucien Bouchard, leader of the Bloc Québécois, dismissed Chrétien's words, calling them "too little, too late."

When the results of the referendum were in, the no side had won, but barely. Over 94 percent of Québec voters had turned out, and just over 50 percent of them had voted no. Québec would stay with Canada, but the results were too close for comfort for many Canadians. Parizeau resigned as premier of Québec and as Parti Québécois leader the day after the referendum—as he had promised to do if the yes side lost—and was replaced by Lucien Bouchard.

After the referendum, talk of Québec sovereignty dwindled. The Québec people seemed tired of the issue and wanted to focus on other areas. The idea has not died, though, and continued to come up from time to time, sometimes gaining a great deal of popularity. In 2004, the leader of the Parti Québécois, Bernard Landry, stated his party's goals as winning the provincial election in 2007 and then winning a separatism referendum in 2008.

In 2000, the federal government passed the Clarity Act, introduced by Prime Minister Chrétien. This act outlined the terms under which Québec would be allowed to separate from Canada. The act stated that future referendum questions must first be submitted to the House of Commons, who would then decide whether or not the questions were clear and understandable. Also, Québec would not be able to separate unless it gained a "clear majority." The act did not define a "clear majority," but Chrétien did say at one point that it would have to be at least more than 50 percent plus one. The terms of Québec sovereignty would not be decided by Québec alone, but by all the provinces together with the First Nations, since a separation of Québec would affect the whole of Canada.

The question of Québec sovereignty affected nearly all Canadian political matters in the early 1990s. Brian Mulroney, prime minister for nine years, experienced such a great loss in popularity in part because he failed to resolve the Québec question. Tensions between separatist parties, such as the Bloc Québécois and the Parti Québécois, and federalist ones, like the Liberal Party, dominated Québec politics. In 1995, the issue came to a crisis point with the Québec Referendum. The narrow margin of victory

Québec's flag

for the no side of the vote showed just how serious the situation was and just how close Canada's unity had come to breaking.

Tensions with Québec separatism were not the only issue of the 1990s, though. Canada's relationship with the United States was an ongoing concern. Brian Mulroney had already introduced the Free Trade Agreement in 1987, but before he left office he had set in motion the plans for an even more far-reaching free trade agreement.

Canada's lumber industry became an
issue in U.S.–Canadian relations.

Three

CANADA AND THE UNITED STATES

The Government of Canada, the Government of the United Mexican States and the Government of the United States of America, resolved to:

STRENGTHEN the special bonds of friendship and cooperation among their nations;

CONTRIBUTE to the harmonious development and expansion of world trade and provide a catalyst to broader international cooperation;

CREATE an expanded and secure market for the goods and services produced in their territories; . . .

CREATE new employment opportunities and improve working conditions and living standards in their respective territories;

UNDERTAKE each of the preceding in a manner consistent with environmental protection and conservation;

PRESERVE their flexibility to safeguard the public welfare;

PROMOTE sustainable development;

STRENGTHEN the development and enforcement of environmental laws and regulations; and

PROTECT, enhance and enforce basic workers' rights

Subsidized means that the government has given money to something.

The North American Free Trade Agreement

One of the final things Brian Mulroney did before he stepped down as prime minister in 1993 was to sign preliminary agreements that would expand the U.S.–Canadian Free Trade

Leaders from Canada, Mexico, and the United States meet to discuss NAFTA.

Agreement to include Mexico. Before his election, Jean Chrétien had been against free trade, but shortly after becoming prime minister he chose to finalize the North American Free Trade Agreement (NAFTA).

Opponents of free trade argued Canada could easily be overwhelmed by American products and American culture. Former prime minister John Turner declared free trade would be harmful to Canadian writers and artists. He was also concerned that Canada could be absorbed into the United States—that giving up economic independence could too easily lead to giving up political independence. With the expansion of free trade to include Mexico, many Canadians also feared Canadians' jobs would be at risk to cheaper Mexican labor.

NAFTA took effect on January 1, 1994, replacing the earlier free trade agreement. Ten years after the original agreement, Canada had formed extremely close trade ties with the United States, and Brian Mulroney argued the deal had been good for Canada. Opponents, however, pointed to Canada's higher unemployment rate. The cultural argument was harder to measure, although many felt the changes would be gradual and could take several more decades to become obvious.

One change brought about by free trade was the arrival of American businesses such as Wal-Mart. In 1994, the company bought 122 Woolco stores in Canada and converted them to Wal-Marts. The presence of Wal-Mart in Canada also contributed to the bankruptcy of Eaton's Company, a department store almost as old as the country itself.

Trade Disputes with the United States

Free trade agreements did not eliminate all disagreements over trade issues. One of the major issues was the controversy over Canadian softwood lumber, the wood used to build houses. American lumber producers felt threatened by cheaper Canadian softwoods, and, in response, the American government imposed high tariffs to even the price. Canadian lumber producers complained that such tariffs were a violation of NAFTA. Americans, on the other hand, claimed that the Canadian government *subsidized* the lumber industry, keeping the prices down.

The dispute, although present for much of the twentieth century, heated up in 1982. The U.S. government, having studied the issue, determined the stumpage fees—those fees paid by lumber companies to cut on government-owned crown land—were too low, therefore serving as a type of government subsidy. Canada disagreed, but the issue did not go away. In 2002, the United States imposed a nearly 19 percent tariff, and then raised it to nearly 30 percent shortly afterward.

Canadians appealed to the NAFTA trade panel several times as well as to the World Trade Organization (WTO) and won nearly all their cases. In 1993, a NAFTA panel said that while low Canadians stumpage fees did act as a subsidy, U.S. tariffs were too high.

Nevertheless, the United States refused to follow the rulings of the courts. Thousands of jobs were lost, mainly in British Columbia, as companies unable to meet the high tariffs closed hundreds of mills.

Another trade dispute involved the Canadian Wheat Board. The Wheat Board, founded during the Great Depression, bought grain from farmers and then sold it. Americans argued that the Wheat Board was subsidized by the Canadian govern-

Canada's wheat farmers felt the effects of NAFTA.

ment and used unfair trading practices. Canadians, however, maintained that the Wheat Board was simply a marketing agent and not a subsidy system. This trade dispute, although not usually as heated as the softwood lumber debates, has also been ongoing during the early twenty-first century.

Other trade issues included Canadian beef, which the United States banned after a Canadian cow tested positive for mad cow disease, and Canada's restrictions on cultural imports such as magazines or television programs. American media is not banned in Canada, but it is governed by a complex set of regulations.

America's Presidents

Canada and its prime ministers have had a varied relationship with U.S. presidents throughout history. Brian Mulroney had a close friendship with President Ronald

Mulroney and the Americans

Brian Mulroney's friendships with both Ronald Reagan and George H. W. Bush were extremely close. In 1987, at the beginning of the free-trade talks, Mulroney serenaded Reagan with "When Irish Eyes Are Smiling." The two fellow Irishmen formed a bond, a bond that was extended to Reagan's successor George Bush. In 2000, Bush and his wife, Barbara, traveled to Canada to attend the wedding of Mulroney's daughter.

Jean Chrétien and George Bush

Reagan and presented one of the eulogies at Reagan's funeral in 2004. When George H. W. Bush took office in 1989, Mulroney also developed a friendship with the new president. The elder President Bush made the first official visit of his presidency to Canada, enthusiastically declaring the friendship between the two countries.

The World According to W

Political cartoon portraying President Bush

Later, Jean Chrétien criticized Mulroney for these relationships, although he himself was close to U.S. president Bill Clinton. When George W. Bush became president in 2001, however, relations between Canada and the United States became strained. Some Canadians felt offended that Bush chose to make his first official trip to Mexico rather than Canada and while there announced Mexico was America's closest friend. Then, after the terrorist attacks of September 11, 2001, in a speech thanking the nations of the world for their outpouring of sympathy and support, Bush failed to thank Canada, to the outrage of many Canadians. One of Chrétien's aides assured Canadians that this omission was not intended to be offensive, but simply meant the United States knew it could count on Canadian support to such an extent that Bush felt he did not even need to mention it.

Part of the strain between the Chrétien–Bush administrations came from the fact that Chrétien was a Liberal prime minister and Bush was a Republican—conservative—president. This meant they found themselves on opposite sides of many issues. Despite a few awkward moments, Chrétien did form a friendship with President Bush, however.

Canada and the Wars on Iraq

On August 2, 1990, Iraq, under its dictator Saddam Hussein, launched a sudden and massive invasion against the tiny country of Kuwait. The reason was oil; Kuwait owned a large portion of the world's oil reserves, and Iraq claimed that some of the oil-producing territory along Kuwait's border actually belonged to Iraq.

The United Nations quickly imposed *economic sanctions* against Iraq and later in the month, authorized the use of force against Iraq if the country did not meet a January 15 deadline to pull out of Kuwait. The United Nations feared Iraq could soon also begin an invasion against Saudi Arabia.

Prime Minister Mulroney quickly committed two Canadian destroyers and a supply ship. Leaders of the Liberal Party and the NDP condemned the move, in part because Mulroney had not consulted Parliament before announcing his intention to send the Canadian ships. The destroyers, the HMCS *Terra Nova* and the HMCS *Athabaskan*, patrolled the Persian Gulf to enforce the economic sanctions, with the supply ship, the HMCS *Protecteur*, giving support to Canadian and other coalition forces. (The coalition was a group of thirty-four countries, led by the United States, who had committed to opposing Iraq.)

The Gulf War

The deadline set for Iraq to leave Kuwait arrived, and nothing happened. The next day, coalition forces declared war on Iraq, beginning the Persian Gulf War. Mulroney defended Canada's support of the war by saying, "If Canada had stood aside we would have betrayed our own national interests, repudiated our own responsibilities, and dishonored our own traditions." Canada's air force participated in the Gulf War, flying combat missions for the first time since the Korean War in the 1950s.

Economic sanctions are trade penalties imposed as a result of breaking a rule or law.

The war lasted for approximately a month and a half. In late February, Iraqi forces began retreating from Kuwait, fleeing back across the border away from coalition troops. On February 27, 1991, the United States declared that Kuwait had been liberated and on March 10, began sending troops home from the Persian Gulf area.

In 2003, a second, more controversial Iraq War began. After the September 11, 2001, terrorist attacks, the United States declared a "war on terror," a general declaration of war against terrorist groups and the countries that shelter them. In 2002, the United States claimed Iraq had failed to get rid of all weapons of mass destruction—as it had been ordered to do after the Persian Gulf War of 1991. UN weapons inspectors had not found stockpiles of weapons, but the United States claimed Iraq had hidden stores. The United Nations refused to authorize the use of force against Iraq, since it had no real evidence the country had any weapons of mass destruction. Despite the lack of UN support, on March 20, 2003, the United States began an invasion of Iraq.

Early in April, the city of Baghdad fell to American forces, followed in the next several days by the cities of Kirkuk and Tikrit. On April 15, President George W. Bush declared the United States victorious, officially ending the war. On December 13, 2003,

Iraq's dictator Saddam Hussein was captured hiding in an underground shelter.

The U.S.-led invasion of Iraq continued to be controversial. Despite President Bush's May 1, 2003, declaration that all major combat operations had been accomplished, conflicts in Iraq went on. American forces remained in Iraq to help a new government establish itself. While some Iraqis were thrilled with the downfall of Saddam Hussein, others hated the Americans and continued to launch guerrilla-style attacks against American soldiers and their allies. The vast majority of Americans killed in Iraq were killed after the official end of the war. As of May 2005, over 1,600 American soldiers had died. Meanwhile, more than 20,000 Iraqis, including civilians, had been killed.

The United States continued its search for weapons of mass destruction in Iraq, but gave up the search in January of 2005, concluding there had been no such weapons after all. Kofi Annan, the UN Secretary-General, later declared that the American invasion had been illegal.

Some countries, such as Britain and Australia, supported the United States in its Iraq invasion, but Canada did not. As a result, American and Canadian relations became strained once more. In April 2003, President Bush cancelled what would have

Political cartoon portraying President Bush's focus on Saddam Hussein, while ignoring North Korean leader

been his first official visit to Canada, claiming he needed to focus on the rebuilding of Iraq. Many Canadians felt, however, his decision was actually based on the fact that Canada had condemned the invasion of Iraq. As the war in Iraq dragged on, anti-American sentiment in Canada grew more common.

Canada's relationship with the United States has gone up and down for centuries. Sometimes, the leaders of the two countries

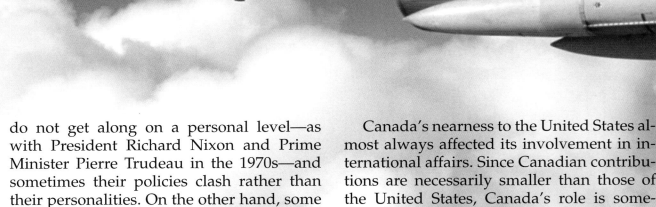

do not get along on a personal level—as with President Richard Nixon and Prime Minister Pierre Trudeau in the 1970s—and sometimes their policies clash rather than their personalities. On the other hand, some prime ministers, such as Brian Mulroney, have been close personal friends with American presidents.

Canada's nearness to the United States almost always affected its involvement in international affairs. Since Canadian contributions are necessarily smaller than those of the United States, Canada's role is sometimes overlooked. In spite of this, Canada has often played an important role in world events.

The Iraq War

Canadian peacekeeping monument in Ottawa

RECONCILIATION

RÉCONC

Four
CANADA AND THE WORLD

In October of 1992, a monument was unveiled in Ottawa on a traffic island in front of the National Gallery. Three bronze soldiers stand atop a high wall, gazing out at the landscape around. The monument, titled *Reconciliation*, was created by artist Jack Harman as a tribute to Canadian peacekeepers.

In 1956, in the face of the Suez Crisis, future prime minister Lester B. Pearson came up with the idea of a UN peacekeeping force. "We need action not only to end the fighting but to make the peace," Pearson said. Since that time, almost 100,000 Canadians have served as UN peacekeepers.

Canadian Peacekeepers

In their decades of contributing forces to the UN peacekeeping troops, Canadians have earned the reputation of courage and honor, for the most part doing their job with hard work and fairness. Canadians have participated in most of the almost sixty UN missions. From 1964 to 1993, Canadians took part in a prolonged peacekeeping mission in Cyprus, finally turning the job over to other UN forces to focus on other missions.

Peacekeeping is a difficult job, and Canada has experienced some failures in the field. In the spring of 1994, for example, UN peacekeepers, under the command of Canadian Roméo Dallaire, failed to

Genocide is the murder of an entire ethnic group.

Post-traumatic stress disorder is a psychological condition that may affect people who have suffered or witnessed severe trauma.

prevent large-scale *genocide* in Rwanda. For years afterward, Dallaire blamed himself for the deaths of so many people, including ten of his own men. After returning to Canada, Dallaire was diagnosed with *post-traumatic stress disorder*. He was discharged from the military in 2000 after being declared unfit to command troops, still suffering emotionally from the events in Rwanda. Slowly, he rebuilt his life, and in 2003, he published a book called *Shake Hands with the Devil* about his experiences in Rwanda.

Canadian peacekeeping forces training in Egypt

The worst moment for Canadian peacekeeping came in 1993, in Somalia. A group of Canadian peacekeepers from the Canadian Airborne Regiment had arrived in Somalia late in 1992. The country had recently faced civil war and famine, and the job of the peacekeepers was to help rebuild and provide relief aid, all while keeping the peace. The problems arose in March of 1993, when Canadians learned of several murders of Somalis by members of the Airborne Regiment. Several had been shot and killed, allegedly while trying to rob the Canadian camp. At least one, however, a sixteen-year-old Somali boy, had been beaten and tortured to death. People throughout the camp heard the boy's screams as he begged for his life saying, "Canada, Canada!" Horrified Canadians back home saw the gruesome photographs the soldiers had taken as mementos.

The investigation and trial dragged on for years. The soldiers had taken home videos of themselves in Somalia, which showed them making racist comments. Reports of other cruelties and mistreatments were heard. One soldier, Kyle Brown, was sentenced to five years in prison for second-degree murder and torture. The soldier featured in the photographs of the torture, Clayton Matchee, attempted suicide shortly after his arrest. He was found unfit to stand trial and committed to a psychiatric institution. Eventually, the entire Airborne Regiment was disbanded, and the Canadian military and peacekeeping troops worked to restore its tainted image.

September 11, 2001

On a sunny Tuesday morning, chaos and horror suddenly erupted in New York City as two hijacked planes slammed into the World Trade Center. Half an hour later, another plane was flown into the Pentagon, which housed the U.S. Department of Defense just outside Washington, D.C. A fourth plane, later thought to be heading toward another Washington target, crashed into a field in Pennsylvania. Canadians, with the rest of the world, watched their televisions in shock and disbelief.

The United States, fearing more attacks, immediately closed its airspace, grounding all flights and turning away airplanes heading into the United States. Canadian airports accepted flights bound for the United States, diverting them to fourteen different Canadian airports. As a security measure, most flights were kept away from the Lester B. Pearson International Airport in Toronto

The September 11 terrorist attack on the United States

59

60

and Dorval International Airport in Montréal, since these were two of the largest airports in Canada.

In all, 255 flights were diverted to Canada, most to Newfoundland, the first province reached by incoming transatlantic flights. Halifax International Airport in Nova Scotia took forty-four planes and Gander International Airport in Newfoundland took thirty-nine. Most of the passengers and many of the pilots did not know what had happened until they landed. For some time, passengers were kept on the airplanes as military personnel scrambled to

Halifax, Nova Scotia

Saying Thank You

For two days, the passengers of the Delta transatlantic flight were welcomed into the homes and hearts of the people of Gander and Lewisporte, Newfoundland. Residents and businesses provided the passengers with food, shelter, telephones, and cable television—all at no charge. When the flight was again in the air and the passengers on their way home to the United States, many discussed how to thank their hosts for all they had done. The passengers decided to establish a scholarship to aid the students of Gander and Lewisporte. Before the flight landed, the passengers and flight crew had pledged $15,000 to the Gander Flight 15 Scholarship Fund. In the first two years of the scholarship program, twenty-nine scholarships were awarded.

make sure no further terrorist threats existed. Even when they were let off the airplanes, there was often nowhere for them to go. In Gander, a town of less than 10,000, 6,600 people were stranded at the airport. People in Gander and neighboring towns took passengers into their homes and provided them with food and shelter.

In the days after the September 11 terrorist attacks, Canadians reeled from the shock. Memorial services were held in all the major cities, as Canadians declared their compassion for those who had lost friends and family members. Nearly three thousand people had been killed—although in those early days, estimates often varied widely, at times guessing numbers nearer to ten thousand. Twenty-four victims were Canadian, but people realized the changes in the world were harder to calculate than the number of casualties. The world held its breath, waiting for more attacks, suspecting even innocent events held threatening possibilities for more death and destruction.

Slowly, as no more attacks came right away, people learned to live again, not forgetting what had happened but moving on with their lives in a world that had changed forever. On the one-year anniversary of the attacks, 2,500 people returned to Gander, Newfoundland, for a memorial service, in part to honor the Newfoundlanders who had given so much to care for the stranded air passengers.

The War on Terror

Shortly after the terrorist attacks on the World Trade Center and the Pentagon, U.S. president George Bush declared a "war on terror." This war would target terrorist groups and the countries that sheltered them. The United States claimed the attacks had been organized by the terrorist group al-Qaeda, headed by Osama bin Laden. Bin Laden was known to have close ties with the Taliban government of Afghanistan.

Only a day after the attacks, the United States invoked Article 5 of the NATO (North Atlantic Treaty Organisation) treaty, the first time this article had been used since the organization formed in 1949. The article states, "The Parties agree that an armed attack against one or more of them in Europe or North America shall be considered an attack against them all," and goes on to say that in the case of such an attack, the other NATO members would take actions to respond, with force if necessary. The purpose of Article 5 had originally been to ensure that the United States would come to the defense of European NATO members if they were attacked by the Soviet Union. Now, the United States had been attacked and had called on its NATO allies to help. Canada was one of those allies.

Despite the NATO agreement, the troops that launched an attack on Afghanistan on October 7, 2001, were not NATO troops, but mainly American forces with British allies. A number of other countries, including Canada, contributed soldiers and aid. These forces succeeded in driving the Taliban out of power, but were not able to discover the location of Osama bin Laden.

On April 18, 2002, an American pilot accidentally bombed a group of Canadian soldiers who were conducting a night-training

Canadian peacekeeping forces in Afghanistan

exercise. Four Canadians were killed and eight wounded, the first Canadians to die in combat since the Korean War. The pilot, who had disobeyed orders to standby until cleared to attack, was first charged with involuntary manslaughter and assault, although these charges were later dropped and he was instead charged with dereliction of duty. Three other Canadian soldiers were later killed in attacks by Afghans.

Canadians are proud of their peacekeeping history.

Humanitarian means committed to improving the lives of other people.

In December 2001, the United Nations approved a peace-keeping force to be sent to Kabul, Afghanistan. The force, known as the International Security Assistance Force, would oversee the transitional government that was in charge of the country after the downfall of the Taliban. In August of 2003, NATO took command of this force. Many of the peacekeepers were Canadian, with over two thousand serving during 2003 and 2004.

Tsunami Relief

On December 26, 2004, a large underwater earthquake occurred off the coast of Indonesia. A shock wave moved out from the site of the earthquake, causing a massive tsunami. As local people went about their daily lives and tourists on Christmas holidays relaxed on the beach, the tsunami struck. In a moment, tens of thousands of people had been washed away. Over a dozen countries were affected, with over 200,000 killed and billions of dollars in damages. Hours after the disaster, Canadian relief workers were on their way to Indonesia, Sri Lanka, and other affected areas. Canadian teams joined with international agencies to coordinate relief efforts. Like many other countries, Canadians personally donated millions of dollars to help the tsunami victims. As of 2005, Canada was continuing to contribute to the rebuilding of the devastated regions.

Internationally, Canada has earned a reputation as one of the best places in the world to live. In fact, the United Nations' list of best places to live ranked Canada first from 1994 to 2000. Although Canada is the second-largest country in the world (Russia is first), its population was only 30 million in 2001, placing it thirty-fifth on the ranking of countries by population.

Canada's contribution to peacekeeping has played a major part in the way the world sees the country. Overall, Canada has a reputation for compassion and honesty. In 1998, Canada helped work out the details for an International Criminal Court (ICC). The ICC would operate under the jurisdiction of the United Nations, prosecuting people for war crimes, genocide, and crimes against humanity. The court was officially established in 2002, and Canadian judge Philippe Kirsch presided over it as president as of May 2005.

Canada is known worldwide for its *humanitarian* action, its peacekeeping forces, and its abundance of unpopulated nature. Often it is compared to the United States. Some think of Canada as similar to the United States but with less people and less crime. Many Americans consider Canada as almost an extension of their own country—although usually a more liberal part. Canadians, on the other hand, at times define themselves by their differences with the United States, a force from which it has been fighting to stay independent since a hundred years before becoming a country.

The new territory of Nunavut

Five

CANADA STEPS INTO THE FUTURE

The quest for their own land began back in 1976. The Inuit of the Northwest Territories, led by John Amagoalik, began requesting the federal government give them their own territory in the eastern part of the region. The Northwest Territories was so huge that the Inuit felt the territorial government in the western city of Yellowknife was not able to satisfactorily address their concerns. The government agreed to consider the idea. The Inuit knew the process would take years. In fact, twenty-three years would pass before the Inuit would get their own territory of Nunavut.

Nunavut

In 1982, the Canadian government held a referendum in the Northwest Territories to determine the level of interest in the creation of a new territory. Across the territories, the result was 56.5 percent in favor of dividing the region. In the east, where the new Inuit territory of Nunavut would be located, the result was 80 percent in favor of division. The majority of no votes came from the white residents of western cities such as Yellowknife, while the western First Nations people generally favored the idea.

In 1993, the Nunavut Land Claims Agreement Act was signed, authorizing the creation of the territory of Nunavut. The Inuit could choose 18 percent of the new territory, while the rest would belong to the Canadian government. Other provisions included hunting rights and a one billion dollar payment paid over fourteen years to the Inuit people.

Even after the signing of the Land Claims Agreement Act, several years passed before Nunavut officially became a territory. On April 1, 1999, the region became Canada's third territory, the thirteenth section to join Confederation. The territory is sparsely populated, with the capital city of Iqaluit having a population of just over five thousand.

Unlike the rest of Canada, Nunavut territorial politicians do not belong to a particular political party. Instead, they each run as independents. After the people have elected members to the Legislative Assembly of Nunavut, these members elect a premier from among themselves. Paul Okalik was chosen to serve as Nunavut's first premier and was reelected in 2004. Nunavut's political system closely mirrors the traditional Inuit leadership councils. Okalik has also set up a group of eleven elders, whose responsibility is to make sure Inuit culture is reflected in the decisions of the Legislative Assembly.

A New Prime Minister

As prime minister, Jean Chrétien had a long-standing rivalry with another Liberal politician, Paul Martin. In the 1990 Liberal leadership convention, Chrétien and Martin had run against each other in an ugly race. After Chrétien had won the leadership of the Liberal Party and in 1993, became prime minister, he appointed Martin to serve as minister of finance. Nevertheless, the relationship between the two men was often tense.

In 2002, Chrétien finally had had enough of Martin and fired him from his position. Martin then announced he would run against Chrétien for leadership of the Liberal Party at the next convention and began traveling across Canada to raise support. Chrétien, realizing he was losing popularity, stated he would resign in the spring of 2004.

A leadership convention was called for in September of 2003, and Martin won without difficulty, with 92 percent of delegate votes. Chrétien had not run, and most of the other candidates had dropped out of the race before the convention. On December 12, 2003, Martin replaced Chrétien as prime minister of Canada.

Shortly after becoming prime minister, Martin called a general election for June of

A citizen of Nunavut

Paul Martin

2004. Many believed Martin could easily win a majority government. In February, however, Canada's auditor general, Sheila Fraser, released a report on a sponsorship program instituted by Chrétien's Liberal government in 1996. The program had been put into operation after the 1995 Québec referendum and was designed to attract the Québec people to the country of Canada through a series of ad campaigns.

After reports of misspent funds, Chrétien had asked Fraser to investigate the program and return a report. Fraser's report, released early in Martin's administration, showed clear misuse of finances. Between 1996 and 2001, 250 million dollars was spent on the program, with nearly 100 million of that going to advertising company fees. Some work had been billed to the government but was never completed. Since Martin had been minister of finance during that time, Canadians immediately began wondering how much he had known about the sponsorship program spending. Martin claimed he had known nothing about it, but people questioned how he could possibly be innocent of wrongdoing.

As a result of the sponsorship scandal, Martin did not win a majority government in the 2004 election, although he did remain prime minister. The Conservative Party of Canada—a merger of the old Progressive Conservative Party and the Canadian Alliance—became the official opposition. The remainder of the seats was split between the Bloc Québécois and the NDP. The Liberals won 135 seats, compared to the 172 won by the other three major parties. This meant Martin would have a more difficult time passing legislation if the opposing parties stood against him.

The sponsorship scandal—sometimes nicknamed AdScam by the media—continued to haunt Martin. Shortly after Fraser released her report, Martin commissioned Justice John Gomery to investigate the sponsorship scandal. Gomery heard testimony from September of 2004 through May of 2005. Information from certain testimonies heard in the Gomery Commission in April of 2005 resulted in a sharp drop in Martin's approval rating. The House of Commons began discussing a vote of no confidence, which would signal the end of Martin's government.

Martin and the United States

Canada's relationship with the United States was often strained during the later years of Chrétien's government. With the election of Martin, some Americans hoped this relationship would become closer. In

Hockey Night in Canada

For over a century, hockey has defined Canada, more recently with hundreds of thousands gathered around their televisions on Saturdays for Hockey Night in Canada. In 2004, though, a contract negotiation between the NHL (National Hockey League) and the NHLPA (National Hockey League Players Association) went bad. With nothing resolved, players refused to take to the ice at the start of the season. By February of 2005, the NHL and NHLPA had still not made any progress toward a settlement, and the NHL was forced to cancel the entire 2004–2005 season. Hockey fans, disgusted with the whole situation, had to find other things to do with their Saturday nights.

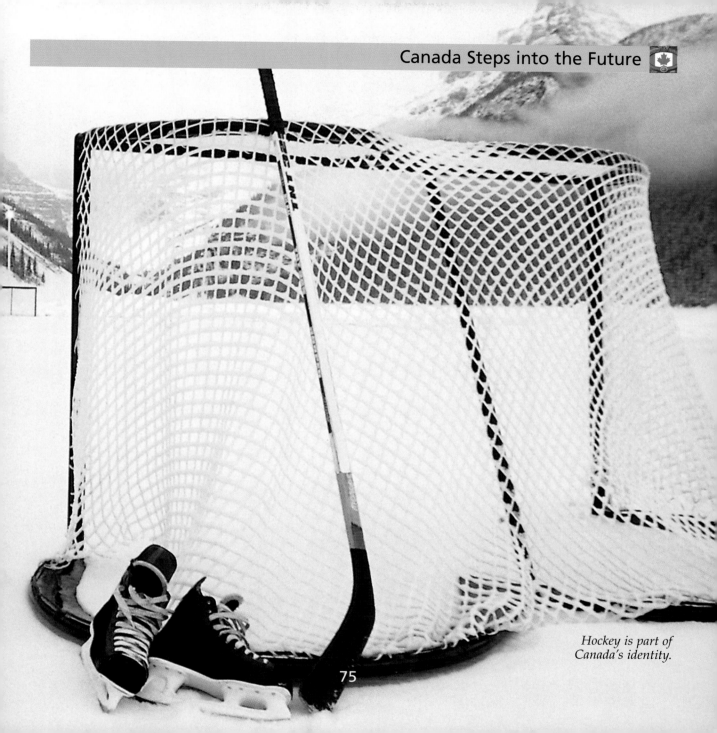

Hockey is part of Canada's identity.

Deployed means readied a military force.

late February of 2005, however, Martin sent Foreign Affairs Minister Pierre Pettigrew to announce Canada would not be taking part in the U.S. missile defense program. The missile defense program, set to become operational later in 2005, would consist of a number of missiles *deployed* along the United States' borders. The missiles would act as a defense if another country were to launch an attack against the United States.

The United States had wanted Canada to participate in the missile defense program, deploying missiles in Canadian territory. Many Canadians assumed Canada would probably take part. Some, though, did approve of Martin's decision, stating he was right to stand up to the United States. More controversial in the United States was Martin's statement that he wanted to be consulted before any missiles were launched over Canadian airspace.

During the last years of the twentieth century, Canada had faced newer versions of the issues it had dealt with since its birth—the relationship between French- and English-speaking Canadians, the relationship between First Nations groups and those with European ancestors, the relationship of Canada with the United States, and the relationship of Canada with the rest of the world. Prime Minister Mulroney had strengthened relations with the United States to an extent previously unknown in Canada, opening up trade relations with the Free Trade Agreement and the North American Free Trade Agreement. In 1995, Québec came a hairsbreadth away from deciding to break away from the rest of Canada. Meanwhile, Canada remained involved in international affairs, specifically in the area of UN peacekeeping.

Canada will undoubtedly continue to deal with forms of these same issues. The Parti Québécois has set a goal of winning a successful sovereignty referendum in 2008. Canadians will struggle with the proximity of the United States, balancing the fascination with American products and media with the desire to maintain a distinct Canadian culture. Internationally, Canada will likely carry on its peacekeeping tradition. Overall, Canadians will keep exploring what it means to be Canadian.

1956 Prime Minister Lester B. Pearson develops the idea for the UN Peacekeeping force.

January 1, 1989 The Free Trade Agreement between Canada and the United States goes into effect.

1987 Meech Lake Accord is formulated.

October 26, 1992 A nationwide vote on the Charlottetown Accord is held.

January 1, 1991 The goods and services tax goes into effect.

1990 The Bloc Québécois Party is formed.

1992 The first ban on cod fishing is declared by the Ministry of Fisheries.

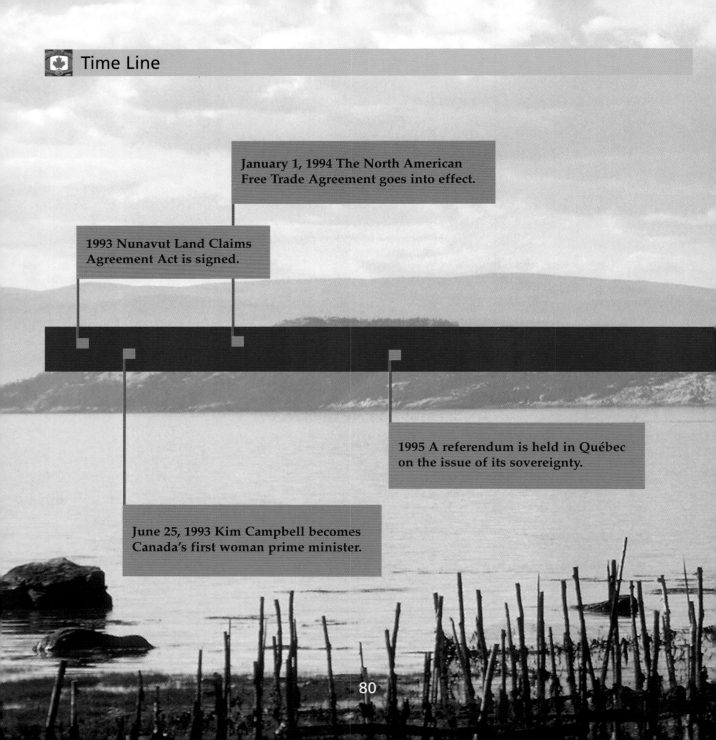

January 1, 1994 The North American Free Trade Agreement goes into effect.

1993 Nunavut Land Claims Agreement Act is signed.

1995 A referendum is held in Québec on the issue of its sovereignty.

June 25, 1993 Kim Campbell becomes Canada's first woman prime minister.

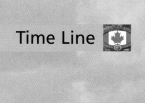

April 1, 1999 Nunavut becomes Canada's third territory.

September 11, 2001 Terrorists attack the United States; twenty-four Canadians are killed.

1998 Canada helps work out the details for the International Criminal Court.

2000 The federal government passes the Clarity Act.

FURTHER READING

Dallaire, Roméo. *Shake Hands with the Devil*. New York: Carroll and Graff, 2004.

DeFede, Jim. *The Day the World Came to Town: 9/11 in Gander, Newfoundland*. New York: HarperCollins, 2003.

Hewson, Martha S. *Defeating Terrorism/Developing Dreams: Beyond 9/11 and the Iraq War*. Northborough, Mass.: Chelsea House, 2004.

Kizilos, Peter. *Quebec: Province Divided*. Minneapolis, Minn.: Lerner Publishing Group, 1999.

Levert, Suzanne. *Canada: Facts and Figures*. Northborough, Mass.: Chelsea House, 2001.

Lutz, Norma Jean. *Nunavut*. Northborough, Mass.: Chelsea House, 2001.

Sanna, Ellyn, and William Hunter. *Canada's Modern-Day First Nations: Nunavut and Evolving Relationships*. Philadelphia, Pa.: Mason Crest, 2006.

Twagilimana, Aimable. *Teenage Refugees from Rwanda Speak Out*. New York: Rosen, 1997.

FOR MORE INFORMATION

Canadian Current Events, Canadian
Broadcasting Company
www.cbc.ca/

Canadian Peacekeeping
www.peacekeeper.ca/

Kim Campbell
www.mta.ca/faculty/arts/
canadian_studies/english/about/
study_guide/famous_women/
kim_campbell.html

Jean Chrétien
www.cbc.ca/news/background/chretien/

Iraq
www.cbc.ca/news/background/iraq/
index.html

The Meech Lake Accord and the
Charlottetown Accord
www.saskschools.ca/curr_content/
history-30/module5/activity4_5.html

Brian Mulroney
www.collectionscanada.ca/
primeministers/h4-3450-e.html

NAFTA
www.dfait-maeci.gc.ca/nafta-alena/
menu-en.asp

Nunavut
www.gov.nu.ca/Nunavut/

The Québec Referendum
educ.queensu.ca/~citc/august99/
quebec_referendum_webquest.htm

Softwood Lumber Dispute
www.cbc.ca/news/background/
softwood_lumber/

Publisher's note:
The Web sites listed on this page were active at the time of publication. The publisher is not responsible for Web sites that have changed their addresses or discontinued operation since the date of publication. The publisher will review and update the Web-site list upon each reprint.

INDEX

patronage 9
Progressive Conservative (PC) Party 9, 11, 22, 32, 33, 34, 73
provincial sales tax (PST) 21, 22

Québec 12, 15, 19, 21, 23–24, 27–32, 36–38

Reform Party 35

separatism 31–32, 38
September 11, 2001 58, 61–63

Trudeau, Pierre 9, 11, 16, 19, 30–31
Turner, John 9, 11

UN peacekeeping troops, Canadian participation in 55–56, 58, 67, 77
Dallaire, Roméo 55–56
Rwanda 56
Somalia 58
United States, Canada's relationship with 11, 39, 51–52, 73, 76–77
presidents, relationship with U.S. 45, 47, 51–52
trade disputes 43–45

war on terror 63, 65
Wells, Clyde 21, 23
World Trade Organization (WTO) 44

PICTURE CREDITS

AFFTC: pp. 52–53

Benjamin Stewart: pp. 8, 20, 68–69, 71, 76

Canadian National Defense: pp: 54–55, 56–57, 64, 65

Canadian Office of the Prime Minister: p. 72

Government of Mexico: p. 42

Manitoba Government: pp. 16–17

National Archives of Canada: pp. 10, 12, 16 (front), 30, 33, 35

National Archives of Canada, Shelley Niro: p. 18 (right),

Photos.com: pp. 1, 13, 14–15, 23, 24–25, 26–27, 28–29, 36–37, 40–41, 44–45, 60–61, 74–75, 78–79, 80–81

Telnaes, Library of Congress: pp. 47, 51

U.S. Army: pp. 48–49

The White House: p. 46

To the best knowledge of the publisher, all other images are in the public domain. If any image has been inadvertently uncredited, please notify Harding House Publishing Service, Vestal, New York 13850, so that rectification can be made for future printings.

BIOGRAPHIES

Sheila Nelson was born in Newfoundland and grew up in both Newfoundland and Ontario. She has written a number of history books for kids and always enjoys the chance to keep learning. She recently earned a master's degree and now lives in Rochester, New York, with her husband and daughter.

SERIES CONSULTANT

Dr. David Bercuson is the Director of the Centre for Military and Strategic Studies at the University of Calgary. His writings on modern Canadian politics, Canadian defense and foreign policy, and Canadian military, among other topics, have appeared in academic and popular publications. Dr. Bercuson is the author, coauthor, or editor of more than thirty books, including *Confrontation at Winnipeg: Labour, Industrial Relations, and the General Strike* (1990), *Colonies: Canada to 1867* (1992), *Maple Leaf Against the Axis, Canada's Second World War* (1995), and *Christmas in Washington: Roosevelt and Churchill Forge the Alliance* (2005). He has also served as historical consultant for several film and television projects, and provided political commentary for CBC radio and television and CTV television. In 1989, Dr. Bercuson was elected a fellow of the Royal Society of Canada. In 2004, Dr. Bercuson received the Vimy Award, sponsored by the Conference of Defence Association Institute, in recognition of his significant contributions to Canada's defense and the preservation of the Canadian democratic principles.